Territory or range is the home area that an anim[...] more common for red foxes to establish territories [...] fall young foxes travel long distances in search of territories of their own, and for many foxes cities provide more food and less danger than the wilderness.

Scavengers are animals that feed on leftovers like garbage or carrion (dead animals). In the wild, scavengers play an important role in keeping the environment clean, but in towns and cities animals that scavenge can become a nuisance.

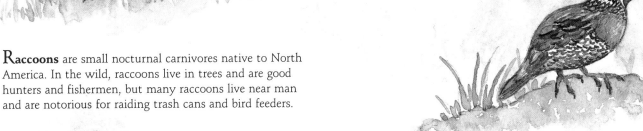

Raccoons are small nocturnal carnivores native to North America. In the wild, raccoons live in trees and are good hunters and fishermen, but many raccoons live near man and are notorious for raiding trash cans and bird feeders.

The **California Quail** is California's state bird. It is a small, plump bird with a black plume on its forehead. It lives among the low plants of the foothills or on the edges of woodlands and eats insects, seeds, buds, and berries. To some people, the call of the California quail sounds like, "You go 'way."

Mule Deer live in western North America and have large furry ears like a mule's. Mule deer are vegetarians and have a stiff-legged walk that allows them to bound over rough trails.

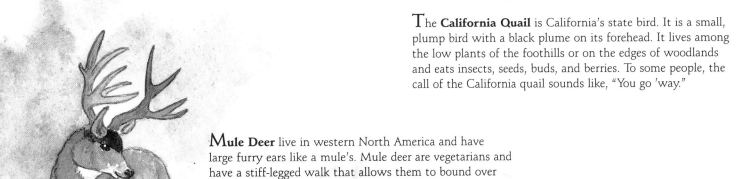

The **California Ground Squirrel** has a dark band of fur that runs from its head down the middle of its back. Including its bushy tail, this squirrel may measure 20 inches in length.

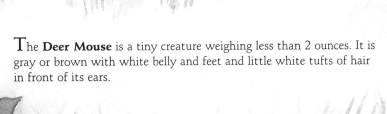

The **Deer Mouse** is a tiny creature weighing less than 2 ounces. It is gray or brown with white belly and feet and little white tufts of hair in front of its ears.

Tessa
On Her Own

Written by **Alyssa Chase**

Illustrated by **Itoko Maeno**

MarshMedia, Kansas City, Missouri

For my father, John Churchill Chase, Jr.,
who is never lazy

Text ©1994 by Marsh Film Enterprises, Inc.
Illustrations ©1994 by Itoko Maeno

First Printing 1994
Second Printing 2000

Published by **MARSH**media

A Division of Marsh Film Enterprises, Inc.
P. O. Box 8082
Shawnee Mission, KS 66208

Library of Congress Cataloging-in-Publication Data
Chase, Alyssa.
     Tessa on her own/written by Alyssa Chase; illustrated
by Itoko Maeno.
          p.   cm.
     Summary: Tessa the fox is too lazy to hunt so she moves
out of the California hills into the town of Ojai, where she can forage
in the city's garbage cans.
     ISBN 1-55942-064-2
     [1. Red fox—Fiction. 2. Foxes—Fiction. 3. Animals—Fiction.
4. Laziness—Fiction.] I. Maeno, Itoko, ill. II. Title.
PZ7.C3853Te 1994   94-8781
[E]—dc20

Book layout and typography by Cirrus Design

Printed in Hong Kong

Special thanks to Donnelle Peyronnin Borgeson
and the Peyronnins of Ojai, California, for their help
with research; to my careful readers, Mary Margaret Obropta,
Trino Boix, and Robert Rebein; and especially to my editor,
Carol Talley, who contributed a great deal to this book.

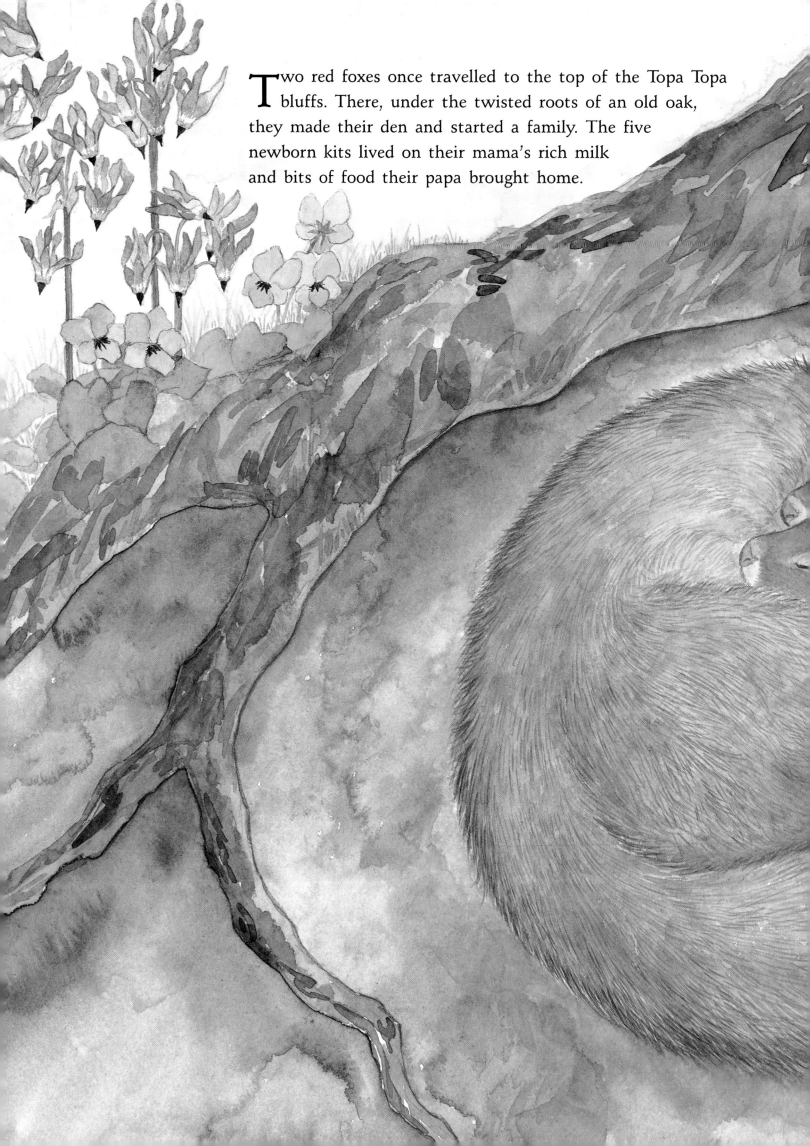

Two red foxes once travelled to the top of the Topa Topa bluffs. There, under the twisted roots of an old oak, they made their den and started a family. The five newborn kits lived on their mama's rich milk and bits of food their papa brought home.

By summertime, the kits were big enough to catch
deer mice and ground squirrels. They had learned
to hunt for themselves. All except a kit named Tessa.

Tessa was lazy. She liked to eat blackberries while
her brother Rex sniffed a rabbit out of a yucca plant
and chased after it with his nose to the ground.
She liked to watch Rex spring into the air and
pounce on his prey, pinning it down with his paws.
Tessa could always talk Rex into sharing his
supper with her.

One day, when the last of the Valencia oranges began
to drop from the trees in the Ojai Valley, Tessa lay in
the sun, half asleep, waiting for lunch.

"Lazy Tessa!" Rex yipped in her ear.

Tessa yawned and stretched, then eyed the squirrel Rex had dropped at her feet. "What have you got there?" she asked. "I'm hungry!"

But instead of sharing, Rex snatched up his catch and bounded down the hill.

"Hey!" Tessa barked. "Where are you going?"
"I'm off to live on my own!" Rex said.
Tessa couldn't believe it! What would she do without Rex? "I'm coming too!" she called.

Rex and Tessa stayed in a grove of sycamore trees. Rex hunted every day and always shared his supper with his sister, which was just fine with Tessa. Then one day Rex didn't bring back any food to share.

"Hey," whined Tessa. "Where's dinner?"

"Tess, you expect too much," said Rex. "It's time you started hunting for yourself. You can't be a lazy fox forever."

"Don't call me lazy," said Tessa.
"And don't tell me what to do."
Tessa was so angry, she trotted off
down the hill, her bright tail
dragging in the dust and snagging
every burr in the brush. "I'm off
to live on my own too!" she
barked over her shoulder.

"I'm not lazy," grumbled Tessa as she made her way down the mountainside. "And I can take care of myself."

But it wasn't so easy being on her own. Nobody wanted to share. "You go 'way," called the quail.

"Get *ouuta* here!" yowled the coyote.

"This is my territory," grunted the buck mule deer.

More than once, Tessa went to sleep hungry. And with so many other animals to wrangle with, she couldn't find a nice place of her own to settle down. Tessa was always on the go.

Then, late one night, she saw something strange.

In the distance, bright little lights sparkled like stars. "That's where I'm going," said Tessa, and she headed on down the hill.

It was almost dawn when Tessa reached the valley below. It was nothing like her old home. There were fences and houses — and chickens. And just when Tessa was wishing that Rex were there to catch a chicken for her, she discovered another new thing — a garbage can — with all kinds of delicious food inside.

Tessa was so busy eating that she didn't see the angry eyes watching her through a black mask.

"Sneaky thief!" squealed the animal. "Why aren't you hunting like a fox?"

"How do you know what foxes do?" said Tessa. She tried to stand tall and look proud, but her muzzle was filthy and her coat was full of burrs.

"I've seen many a fox in my time," said the raccoon, "and every last one of them was a hunter. What kind of a lazy rascal are you — scavenging a poor raccoon's supper?" The raccoon laughed, and her three masked pups laughed with her.

It became a contest getting to all the town garbage cans before the bandit raccoons. "What right does a raccoon have to call a *fox* a thief?" Tessa thought as she gobbled down one tasty scrap after another.

One rainy November evening, the smell of roast turkey drew Tessa to a dark corner near a restaurant. But she stopped short when she caught a whiff of something besides turkey — danger! Then she heard a cry.

"Help us, fox!"

It was the raccoon and her pups, trapped in a wire cage. Tessa took a few careful steps toward them. Just then, a man came out of the restaurant, got into the truck, and drove away, taking the raccoons with him.

All Tessa could do was watch.

Now Tessa had the garbage cans all to herself. She didn't have to race the raccoons to get to the best food.

"I wish Rex could see me now," she thought.

One night, Tessa wandered into an alley where she had never been before. She sniffed fresh food, and the scent was coming from a big dumpster. Tessa tiptoed up to a rusty hole on one side. Her nose wiggled. "Something in there sure smells good!" she whispered. Tessa squeezed through the hole.

Inside Tessa found delicious meats of all shapes and sizes. She gorged herself like she'd never done before. But when it was time to go, Tessa couldn't squeeze her full belly back through the rusty hole!

She peeked out and saw a rat scuttling by. "Help!" she said, "I'm stuck!" The rat snickered in Tessa's face.

"What rat would help a fox?" he said with an evil smile. He bit Tessa on the nose and disappeared down a dark hole.

Tessa was miserable. Her nose hurt, she felt sick, and now she was trapped — just like the raccoons!

Hours passed before daylight crept under the heavy dumpster lid. The day grew warmer, and the food in the dumpster began to spoil. The rotten smell reminded Tessa of all the days and nights she'd spent scavenging her meals from garbage cans.

From the rusty hole Tessa watched a tomcat run by chasing a mouse. "I have been lazy," she mumbled to herself. "Foxes hunt. That's what Rex said, and the raccoon said it too. How can I call myself a fox? If I ever get out of here, I'm going to build a beautiful den and hunt for my supper."

Tessa dozed on her garbage heap until late in the evening. A creaky sound woke her, and a narrow shaft of light streamed into her prison, then widened. Blinking her eyes, Tessa saw a hand — then an arm.

Tessa leapt as high as she could over the side of the dumpster, tumbled to the ground, and scrambled into the brush.

When she finally stopped to rest it was morning, and she was on a quiet hillside under shady trees. "This will be my new territory," Tessa thought. She found an abandoned burrow and worked all morning digging a new den near an oak tree — just like her family's old home.

At first, Tessa could barely catch enough to keep herself from starving, but in time, she became an excellent hunter. Tessa felt proud to be a fox.

"Nobody can call me lazy now!" she said, carefully grooming her full, russet tail.

One day, Tessa caught the scent of another fox.

She was sure it was a dog fox, especially when she saw his handsome, bushy tail waving in the tall grass.

"I'm Tristan," he said, stepping out to meet Tessa. "Would you like to hunt with me?"

Tessa and Tristan hunted
together that day, and every day
after that until blossoms filled the
pomegranate trees and lupines and poppies
waved in the breeze.

Then one fine spring day, Tessa lay down in
the den and let Tristan do the hunting for her.

Now Tessa was busy with a *new* kind of work.

Dear Parents and Educators:

When we are very young, we must rely on others to take care of us, to do the work necessary for our survival — just as Tessa relies on her parents to provide her with milk and bits of food. As we grow older, however, we begin to learn the skills we will need to take care of ourselves, and — with effort and determination — we eventually achieve a level of competence that allows us to live "on our own." Only when we are able to take care of ourselves can we form sturdy partnerships with others and take care of our own young ones.

If we do not develop our survival skills, then we must remain dependent upon others for the fruits of their labors — or eke out an uncertain and inadequate livelihood. This is what Tessa discovers. She believes that — like her accomplished brother Rex — she can live on her own, but without his skills of stalking, chasing, and pouncing, her independence is illusory.

After spending a night trapped in a garbage dumpster, Tessa finally realizes that she must work to live successfully. In time she learns to take care of herself and of others.

Here are some questions you might ask to help children think about the message of ***Tessa on Her Own:***

- How do Tessa's mother and father take care of her and the other kits?
- What skills do the kits learn as they grow older?
- Why doesn't Tessa learn to hunt?
- Was Tessa prepared to live on her own?
- In what ways do other people take care of you?
- In what ways are you able to care for yourself?
- Will someone take care of you when you are grown up?
- What kind of work might you like to do when you grow up?

Available from MarshMedia

These storybooks, each hardcover with dust jacket and full-color illustrations throughout, are available at bookstores, or you may order by calling MarshMedia toll free at 1-800-821-3303.

Amazing Mallika, written by Jami Parkison, illustrated by Itoko Maeno. 32 pages. ISBN 1-55942-087-1.

Bailey's Birthday, written by Elizabeth Happy, illustrated by Andra Chase. 32 pages. ISBN 1-55942-059-6.

Bastet, written by Linda Talley, illustrated by Itoko Maeno. 32 pages. ISBN 1-55942-161-4.

Bea's Own Good, written by Linda Talley, illustrated by Andra Chase. 32 pages. ISBN 1-55942-092-8.

Clarissa, written by Carol Talley, illustrated by Itoko Maeno. 32 pages. ISBN 1-55942-014-6.

Emily Breaks Free, written by Linda Talley, illustrated by Andra Chase. 32 pages. ISBN 1-55942-155-X.

Feathers at Las Flores, written by Linda Talley, illustrated by Andra Chase. 32 pages. ISBN 1-55942-162-2.

Following Isabella, written by Linda Talley, illustrated by Andra Chase. 32 pages. ISBN 1-55942-163-0.

Gumbo Goes Downtown, written by Carol Talley, illustrated by Itoko Maeno. 32 pages. ISBN 1-55942-042-1.

Hana's Year, written by Carol Talley, illustrated by Itoko Maeno. 32 pages. ISBN 1-55942-034-0.

Inger's Promise, written by Jami Parkison, illustrated by Andra Chase. 32 pages. ISBN 1-55942-080-4.

Jackson's Plan, written by Linda Talley, illustrated by Andra Chase. 32 pages. ISBN 1-55942-104-5.

Jomo and Mata, written by Alyssa Chase, illustrated by Andra Chase. 32 pages. ISBN 1-55942-051-0.

Kiki and the Cuckoo, written by Elizabeth Happy, illustrated by Andra Chase. 32 pages. ISBN 1-55942-038-3.

Kylie's Concert, written by Patty Sheehan, illustrated by Itoko Maeno. 32 pages. ISBN 1-55942-046-4.

Kylie's Song, written by Patty Sheehan, illustrated by Itoko Maeno. 32 pages. (Advocacy Press) ISBN 0-911655-19-0.

Minou, written by Mindy Bingham, illustrated by Itoko Maeno. 64 pages. (Advocacy Press) ISBN 0-911655-36-0.

Molly's Magic, written by Penelope Colville Paine, illustrated by Itoko Maeno. 32 pages. ISBN 1-55942-068-5.

My Way Sally, written by Mindy Bingham and Penelope Paine, illustrated by Itoko Maeno. 48 pages. (Advocacy Press) ISBN 0-911655-27-1.

Papa Piccolo, written by Carol Talley, illustrated by Itoko Maeno. 32 pages. ISBN 1-55942-028-6.

Pequeña the Burro, written by Jami Parkison, illustrated by Itoko Maeno. 32 pages. ISBN 1-55942-055-3.

Plato's Journey, written by Linda Talley, illustrated by Itoko Maeno. 32 pages. ISBN 1-55942-100-2.

Tessa on Her Own, written by Alyssa Chase, illustrated by Itoko Maeno. 32 pages. ISBN 1-55942-064-2.

Thank You, Meiling, written by Linda Talley, illustrated by Itoko Maeno. 32 pages. ISBN 1-55942-118-5.

Time for Horatio, written by Penelope Paine, illustrated by Itoko Maeno. 48 pages. (Advocacy Press) ISBN 0-911655-33-6.

Toad in Town, written by Linda Talley, illustrated by Itoko Maeno. 32 pages. ISBN 1-55942-165-7.

Tonia the Tree, written by Sandy Stryker, illustrated by Itoko Maeno. 32 pages. (Advocacy Press) ISBN 0-911655-16-6.

Companion videos and activity guides, as well as multimedia kits for classroom use, are also available. MarshMedia has been publishing high-quality, award-winning learning materials for children since 1969. To order or to receive a free catalog, call 1-800-821-3303, or visit us at www.marshmedia.com.

The **Red Fox** is a species of fox found in North America, Asia, Europe, and Australia. Red foxes are exceptional eyesight, hearing, and so at avoiding man. That's why scient the behavior of red foxes in the wil always had a reputation as a sly tric 31/2 feet long from the tip of the no and can live up to 14 years. Male fo foxes, female foxes are called vixens foxes can be called pups, cubs, whe

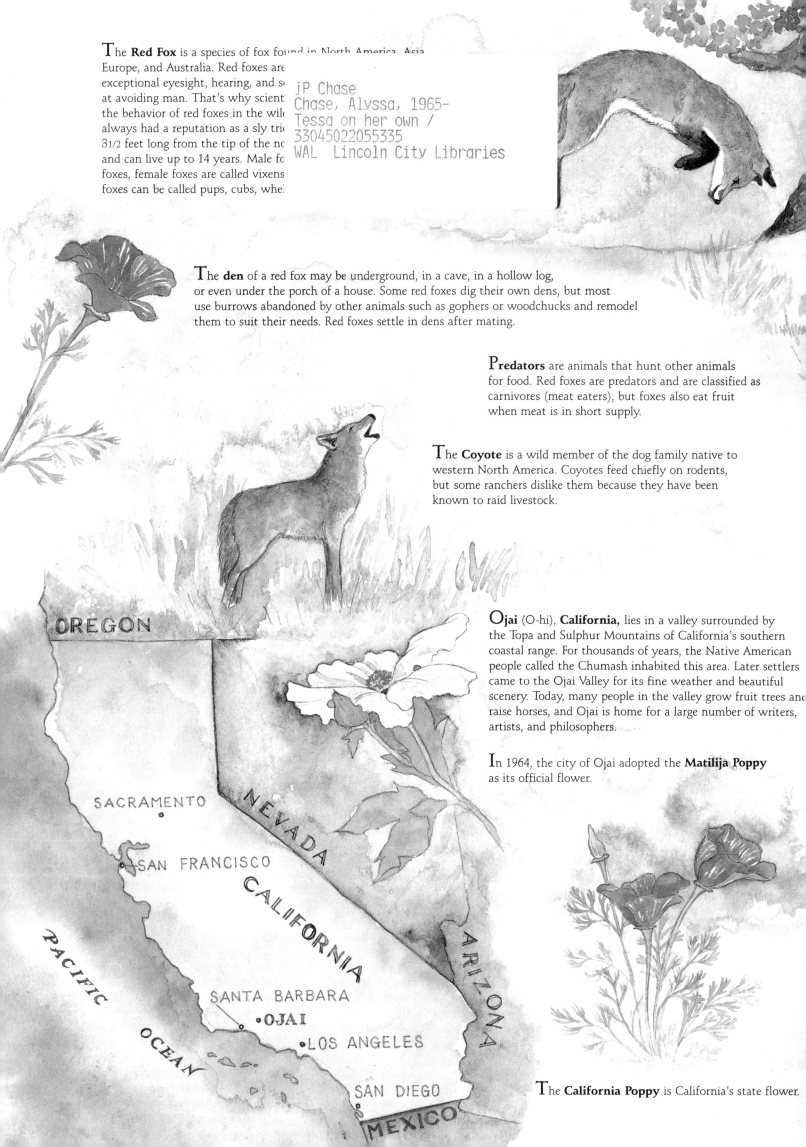

The **den** of a red fox may be underground, in a cave, in a hollow log, or even under the porch of a house. Some red foxes dig their own dens, but most use burrows abandoned by other animals such as gophers or woodchucks and remodel them to suit their needs. Red foxes settle in dens after mating.

Predators are animals that hunt other animals for food. Red foxes are predators and are classified as carnivores (meat eaters), but foxes also eat fruit when meat is in short supply.

The **Coyote** is a wild member of the dog family native to western North America. Coyotes feed chiefly on rodents, but some ranchers dislike them because they have been known to raid livestock.

Ojai (O-hi), **California,** lies in a valley surrounded by the Topa and Sulphur Mountains of California's southern coastal range. For thousands of years, the Native American people called the Chumash inhabited this area. Later settlers came to the Ojai Valley for its fine weather and beautiful scenery. Today, many people in the valley grow fruit trees and raise horses, and Ojai is home for a large number of writers, artists, and philosophers.

In 1964, the city of Ojai adopted the **Matilija Poppy** as its official flower.

OREGON

SACRAMENTO

SAN FRANCISCO

NEVADA

PACIFIC OCEAN

CALIFORNIA

SANTA BARBARA
•OJAI
•LOS ANGELES

ARIZONA

SAN DIEGO

MEXICO

The **California Poppy** is California's state flower.